# It Goes Eeeeeeeeeeeee!

# It Goes Eeeeeeeeeeeee!

## Jamie Gilson

*Illustrated by Diane de Groat*

Clarion Books

NEW YORK

Clarion Books
a Houghton Mifflin Company imprint
215 Park Avenue South, New York, NY 10003

www.houghtonmifflinbooks.com

Printed in the U.S.A.

Book design by Carol Goldenberg

*Library of Congress Cataloging-in-Publication Data*
Gilson, Jamie.
It goes Eeeeeeeeeeee! / by Jamie Gilson ; illustrated by Diane de Groat.
p.    cm.
Summary: Patrick, the new boy in Richard's class, is always causing trouble,
but his work on a science project about bats helps him make new friends.
ISBN 0-395-67063-2    PA ISBN 0-618-05155-4
[1. Schools—Fiction. 2. Bats—Fiction. 3. Friendship—Fiction]
I. De Groat, Diane, ill.    II. Title
PZ7.G4385Yq 1994
[Fic]—dc20                93-559
CIP
AC

WOZ 10 9

*Special thanks to Scott Heinrichs,*
*Lincoln Park Zoo, Chicago*

For more information about bat houses write:
Bat Conservation International
P.O. Box 162603
Austin, TX 78716-2603

*To Gail Forsberg
and the Pretty Goods*

# Contents

# 1.

**Pow! Pow!**

"Don't look at him," Ben whispered. "If you don't look, he'll go away."

I jumped in a puddle. So did Ben. We jumped so hard, mud splashed our chins.

"I can do that," Patrick called. He was standing across the street from my house. "I'm coming over."

"You can't play with Richard and me," Ben called back. "We're busy."

Ben ran his fingers through the mud.

I pulled my Cubs cap way down over my eyes. I tried to pretend that Patrick wasn't there.

Ben is my best friend always. Patrick is new. We're supposed to be nice to him, but it's hard. Patrick is trouble.

"There's a fat worm," Ben said. "By your toe. Grab it."

Ben likes worms and bugs a lot. I think they're ooshy. I picked it up, anyway, and dropped it in the grass.

"That's worm number five," I told him. "Can we stop now?" A mosquito buzzed me and I slapped it.

"No!" he said. "Here's number six." He fished one out of the mud and put it in his T-shirt pocket.

"Let's go inside," I said. "It's going to rain again, and the mosquitoes are eating my ears."

"We can't," he told me. "These worms are in big danger."

It was Endangered Animal Month in Mrs. Zookey's class. Everybody had to choose one. Mine was the humpback whale. Ben had the baboon. Nobody had worms.

But Ben said you could die if you're a sidewalk worm. People might step on you. Or you might drown.

"Give me your calculator," he said.

I got a calculator for my birthday. It's shaped like a dinosaur, but it works, anyway. Every morning I put it in my pants pocket because you never can tell when you'll need to figure something out. I gave it to him.

"OK," he said. "What if we save thirteen worms an hour? And what if we're out here three hours?"

"If we're out here three hours, I'll be one big mosquito bite."

"No, I mean, how many worms would we save?" He punched $3 \times 13 =$. "It's thirty-nine! We save *thirty-nine* worms in just three hours."

He tossed me the calculator. "Sure," I said, "and if we kept it up for twenty-four hours . . ." I pushed $24 \times 13 =$. "We could find *three hundred twelve* worms. We would also miss school Monday." I slipped the dinosaur back in my pocket.

"There!" He pointed. "Look in the crack! Worm seven!"

"Pow!" we heard. "I got it! Pow! Pow!"

It was Patrick. With three fat squirts of water he had turned worm number seven to mush.

"That was mean," Ben yelled. "Did a worm ever hurt you?"

Patrick waved his huge yellow water gun in the air. It looked like Super Squirt from Outer Space.

"Ha!" he said. "I'm an excellent shot."

Patrick thinks he's best. And he says so. He wears a suit with a bow tie. To school. With shiny leather shoes. And he always wants to play with us. Patrick is a pest.

"You like my gun?" he asked, holding it up. "My

uncle gave it to me. My mom says I can't keep it, but I will. I can do whatever I want to. What're you doing?"

"Saving worms," I told him.

"They're endangered," Ben explained.

"That's dumb," Patrick said. "Endangered means there aren't many left and they all could die forever. Like the dinosaurs and the dodos did. But there are lots and lots of worms. You don't know *that?*"

"I know there are two of us," Ben told him, "and there's only one of you. You better not call us dumb."

"Ha," Patrick said. He aimed his squirt gun at a long, yucky worm.

Before he could mush it to pieces, I grabbed the worm and dropped it in the grass.

Something moved. Something was in the grass where the worm fell. It was small and brown.

"Hey, Ben," I called, "what's this?" I turned the bill of my cap around so I could see better.

Ben came to look. "A leaf, maybe," he said.

It was too fat for a leaf. And part of it was furry.

I pulled some grass and brushed the fur with it. "A mouse got caught in the rain," I said.

Patrick came to look, too.

The brown thing shook.

"Is it alive?" he asked.

"Maybe."

"It's a mouse," Ben said, "but a cat bit its tail off."

"I think it's a baby bird," I told them. "See the wings."

But its wings didn't look like bird wings. They didn't have feathers. They looked like paper-thin brown leather.

It was breathing.

Patrick took three giant steps back. "I know what that is," he said, "and I'm going to shoot it dead." He raised his water gun.

"Don't you dare," I told him. "It isn't hurting you."

"Ha! That's what you think." He aimed.

"Go away, Patrick." Ben told him. "You're trouble."

"I am not," Patrick said. "I know what I know."

He zapped Ben's heel with water.

"You want a worm down your back?" Ben asked him.

"If we blow on it," I told them, "maybe it'll wake up and fly away."

"It better not." Patrick aimed again.

I took off my cap and covered the bird-mouse to keep it from getting wet.

6

"OK," Patrick said, backing up some more. "But don't say I didn't tell you. I know what I know."

I put my cap back on. Ben kneeled down, and we both looked at the small furry thing in the grass.

"If you don't watch out," Patrick called, "it'll bite you in the neck." He tucked his water gun under his arm. "Then your eyes will start to glow like red light bulbs and you'll grow long fangs. And then every night at midnight you'll fly out and bite people and they'll bleed real blood."

"Sure." Ben laughed.

A mosquito landed on my arm. I whacked it. It made a blob of real blood.

"I know what I know," Patrick said.

The thing in the grass moved. We watched. It raised its head. Its wings began to open.

"Run," Patrick called. The wings opened wide.

I had seen those wings before. They were Halloween wings.

Ben caught his breath. I could tell he knew them, too. They were wings you see in ads for scary movies.

But they were real, and they were going to fly.

"It's a . . . bat," I whispered.

"Run," Patrick called again.

And we ran.

## 2.

# Knock Knock

"Faster," Patrick called. He covered his head with his arms. "It'll land in your hair!"

I held my cap on tight. I ran faster. We raced up the steps to my porch.

My heart was going bump, bump, bump. "Is it after us?" I asked.

Nobody looked.

We ran inside.

We ran into my room and slammed the door.

Then we stood between my bed and the door, breathing hard.

"Richard," Mom called from the kitchen. "Please don't slam the door. It makes the house shake."

My closet was open, so I ran inside. Ben came,

too. Patrick threw his water gun on my bed and pushed in with us. He slammed the door behind him.

It was dark in the closet, and it smelled like wet socks.

We waited for the bat to come.

"It'll bite us for sure. And turn us into vampires," Patrick whispered. "I know."

He sounded like he did know.

"Will it take a worm instead?" Ben asked. "I've got one in my pocket."

My knees felt funny. The closet was dark and hot.

I scratched an itchy bump on my neck. Maybe it was a mosquito bite and maybe it wasn't.

Vampires in movies have fangs. I ran my tongue across my teeth. They felt sharper than when I ate spaghetti at lunch.

The closet was tight. Patrick kept stepping on my toes. I hoped Ben's worm wouldn't get squooshed.

"You really think it came after us?" I asked.

"It could have flown *in* with us," Patrick said.

He was right. I opened the door fast. No bat flew out.

We flew out.

Nothing was in the air. But we listened.

Something brushed against the window.

"That's just a branch," I told them. "It hits the glass sometimes."

"Ha!" Patrick said. "That's what you think."

My window was open. It was only open a little, but I closed it all the way. And that wasn't to keep out the rain, either. But it was raining. And the wind was blowing hard.

"Bats get stuck in your hair," Patrick told us. "They hide in it and they won't come out. They can't come out. You know why? They're blind as a bat."

I'd heard people say that. Maybe Patrick did know.

I knew about bats, too. "Mostly," I told them, "bats live in haunted houses with all-black cats. They fly out on Halloween night."

"They come out other times, too," Patrick said, soft and scary. "Like right . . . NOW!"

I got goose bumps on my arms. Or maybe they were bat bumps.

"Where did it come from?" I asked. "Are we near a ghost house?"

"I think it followed Patrick here," Ben said. "I never saw one before."

"In the zoo, I did," Patrick told us. "But they were locked up behind glass so they couldn't get you. A red light was on. They were sleeping upside down."

We listened to the thunder rumble and watched the leaves brush the window.

"Let's play Bat. They go like this," Patrick said. He stuck his teeth out over his bottom lip. "I'll be the bat." He waved his arms like they were wings. Then he ran at Ben and me like he was going to bite us.

"I don't want to play Bat," I said. But I chased him back, anyway.

He climbed on my bed and jumped up and down. His arms were flapping.

"Cut it out, Patrick," I said.

He jumped off the bed. "I'm the biggest, baddest bat in the world," he yelled.

Ben grabbed a pillow and swung it at him. I threw my cap, but it missed.

*Knock knock.*

Something was hitting my door. Even Patrick got quiet.

*Knock.*

Patrick climbed on my bed.

*Knock.*

What if it was the bat, trying to get in?

Patrick began to bounce up and down. He was yelling, "Bats, bats, big as cats. Bats, bats, bite like rats. Bats, bats . . ."

*Knock knock.* It was louder.

Could a real, live, biting bat be any worse than Patrick?

I didn't care what was knocking. I didn't care if it was a *Tyrannosaurus rex*. I turned the knob and opened the door wide.

"What *are* you boys doing?"

It was not a bat. It was not a *Tyrannosaurus rex*. It was my mother. She was not happy.

"OK, Richard," she said, "outside you go. It's stopped raining. You boys have more energy than one small room can hold."

Ben and I ran straight to the front door and looked out the screen at the sky. All of the monsters were hiding.

Patrick followed us. "If you hop five steps and run three, bats won't get you. That's one thing I know."

He opened the door and hopped down the steps. "One. Two. Three. Four. Five. I saw a bat alive." He ran. "One. Two. Three. He won't catch me."

Then he turned around.

"I forgot," he said. "My mother won't let me keep the gun. So I left it on your bed. I'll just play with it here every day."

"Trouble," I told Ben.

We watched Patrick go. He didn't look to see if the bat was back.

We put our hands on our heads. We hopped down the steps. Ben scooped the worm out of his pocket. It was still wiggling. He dropped it in the grass.

Then we crossed our fingers and ran to the place where the bat had been.

It was gone.

## 3.

# Flat Rat Fat Cat

*T*he bat was still gone in the morning. On my way to the school bus, I hopped five steps and ran three, over and over. And I wore my cap, just in case. I saw some worms, but no bats.

I had Patrick's yellow squirt gun with me. It was dry. It was dry because all of its water had leaked into my bed. My sheets were soaked.

I told my mom so she wouldn't think I did it.

Mom said to get that gun out of the house. She said no way I could keep it one day more.

So, I stuck it in a plastic bag and took it with me. You can't have squirt guns at school, but Patrick could hide it.

The bus was packed. Nobody noticed the plastic bag.

It was fifth grade Science Fair day. A lot of the big kids were carrying their science stuff. One girl had plants on the seat beside her. A boy was holding a box of bottles with flowers sticking out of them. Another kid took up the whole front seat with something that looked like a rocket.

All of the places were full but one. I didn't want to sit in that one. It was the seat next to Patrick.

"My mother won't let me keep this," I told him, and gave him the bag. I didn't tell him it wet my bed. He'd go *Ha!* a billion times if I told him that. I looked for another seat.

Mostly I sit with Ben, but he was with his brother Morgan, who's in fifth. Ben had a cage in his lap.

"I've got Lettuce," Ben called. "See?" Lettuce is one of Ben and Morgan's gerbils. Gerbils are not endangered animals. Ben and Morgan started with two. Now they have twelve. Eleven of them are called Fluffy, and one of them is called Lettuce.

Lettuce is the one that comes when Morgan blows a whistle.

"Morgan is bringing Lettuce for his Yummies and Yuckies," Ben told me. Yummies and Yuckies is what our teacher, Mrs. Zookey, calls show-and-tell.

"It's for Science Fair," Morgan said, and he bopped Ben on the head with a notebook.

I looked again for a place to sit. Dawn Marie and Linda were sharing the seat in front of Patrick. They're at Table Two with Ben and me in Mrs. Zookey's room. We're all friends.

"OK, Richard, so sit," the bus driver called. "If you don't sit, you're going to do a back flip and a belly flop."

Dawn Marie and Linda giggled.

I crossed my eyes at them and sat down next to Patrick. He was all dressed up in his suit and bow tie.

"Did the vampire keep you awake?" he asked me.

"No way," I said. I lied. Two times I woke up. Two times I was sure I heard it brush the window.

"I brought a Yucky to school today," he said. "It's in here." He put his hand over his coat pocket, like he thought I'd try to steal what was inside.

"Shhhhhh," he told his pocket, but I didn't hear anything.

"What's in there?" I asked. "It isn't alive, is it?" Mrs. Zookey won't let us bring live things without asking her first.

16

Patrick smiled like he had a secret. Then he stuck his top teeth over his bottom lip and flapped his arms.

"It's not that," I told him. "I bet it's not."

He smiled bigger. "Want to see?" he asked.

I bent over his pocket.

"Watch out!" he yelled. I pulled back. Dawn Marie and Linda turned to look. Patrick laughed.

"It won't bite you if I tell it not to," he said. "Guess what it is. Guess."

I pulled my Cubs cap down and looked out the window.

"It's not a big fat rat and it's not a flat cat," he said. "Fat-rat-flat-cat, fat-rat-flat-cat. Can you say that fast?"

"Hey, Richard, guess what," Ben yelled back. "Lettuce has already chewed up one whole toilet paper tube. We put it in the cage just before we left. Morgan brought ten toilet paper tubes with him for his science experiment."

Morgan bopped Ben on the head again.

Linda turned around. "Richard, I have a math problem. If I've got seven cans of beans and you take five of them, how many do I have left?"

That was easy. I didn't even need my calculator. "Two cans," I told her.

Linda and Dawn Marie laughed. "Toucans—those are my endangered animals," Linda said.

Patrick laughed with them. "Ha! Richard and Ben are doing earthworms," he said, and he laughed a whole lot.

Linda and Dawn Marie didn't laugh with him.

"They are not," Dawn Marie said.

"We sit with them at Table Two," Linda told him, "and we know better."

"I bet I've got the best Yucky today," Patrick said.

"Bet you don't," Dawn Marie told him. She and Linda looked at each other, rolled their eyes, and turned away.

Patrick stopped smiling. "This isn't as good as my old school," he said. "Nobody at this school likes me."

He hugged the plastic bag. Then he looked up.

"You know what?" he said. "I've got a secret. I've got a funny Yummy. Everybody will laugh." He grinned. "I bet everybody will like me today."

The bus pulled up at school, and all the fifth graders got off with their projects. The rest of us piled out next. Ben got to carry Lettuce's cage to the fifth grade room.

I walked with Patrick.

"Since you're my best friend," he said, "I'm going to tell you my secret. And I'm going to show you what's in my pocket. Ready? One. Two . . ."

Maybe he'd make it bite me. I didn't want to know his secret. I ran ahead. I didn't want to be Patrick's friend. At least he didn't sit with us at Table Two.

## 4.

## Plop

"I've got scabs on *both* my knees," Dawn Marie said, looking straight at Patrick. "It was the yuckiest. There was blood all over the sidewalk. See?" She pointed.

We saw. Dawn Marie was standing on a chair in front of the room. She was showing off her skinned knees to Mrs. Zookey's whole second grade class.

We had already done the Pledge of Allegiance and lunch count. Now Dawn Marie was the first one up for Yummies and Yuckies.

We do Yummies and Yuckies almost every morning. You've got to tell if what you're showing is a good or a bad thing.

"It's a *fake* thing," Patrick called from Table One. "You put red marker on your knee, that's all," he went on. "Look, everybody, Dawn Marie's faking!"

"No way," Dawn Marie told him. "That's medicine, red medicine. My father put it on."

"Right," Patrick said, like he knew it wasn't.

"That's enough, Patrick," Mrs. Zookey warned him. Patrick may know a lot, but people always have to tell him when enough is.

Dawn Marie kept going. "Also, I've got an excellent Yummy. But I'll save it for tomorrow."

She had to save it. Mrs. Zookey won't let us do more than one at a time.

"I'll give you a clue, though," she went on. "It's an animal. And its knees don't bend like ours. They don't do this." She kicked her bottom with her heel. "Its knees face *back*, so it could kick its belly with its toes—if it wanted to. I don't know if it skins its knees."

"It must walk really, really funny," somebody at Table Three said.

"It doesn't walk," Dawn Marie told her. "It flies."

"Ah, yes," Mrs. Zookey said. "The only flying mammal. I hope you're not planning to bring one to class."

"Oh, no," Dawn Marie said. "It wouldn't like it here at all."

"Dawn Marie should sit down," Ben said. "It's not fair." He waved his arm high so Mrs. Zookey would choose him. "I'm going to tell about Lettuce being at school," he whispered.

"I'm next," I said, and raised my hand, too. I wanted to tell about the bat. It would be the biggest Yucky of all time.

At Table One Patrick was standing on his chair shaking both arms. "Me!" he yelled. "Mrs. Zookey, call on me!"

"Patrick, get down off that chair at once," she said. "All right, everyone calm down. Fold your hands on your desks, and count to ten without moving your lips."

*Onetwothreefourfivesixseveneightnineten.*

Ben and I raised our hands again. So did just about everybody else.

"I want to say how Lettuce is in school chewing up toilet paper tubes. Me first." Ben pushed my arm down.

"*I* want to say how a big black bat almost turned my eyes to red light bulbs." Ben is my best friend but sometimes he makes me mad. "You make me mad," I told him.

He pushed me.

I pushed him back.

"Richard," Mrs. Zookey said, and I got ready to

23

go to the front of the room. "Richard, Ben, that's enough of that." She crossed her arms and looked at us.

At Table One, Patrick was throwing his arm, calling, "Me, please, me."

"Tell us, Patrick," Mrs. Zookey said. "Do you really have something wonderful?"

"The best," Patrick told her. Then he turned around so the class couldn't see what he was doing.

The kids at Table One were laughing. They could see. This must be what Patrick said would be funny. This must be what he said would make everybody like him.

Patrick picked up the plastic sack I'd given him and walked to the front of the class. He waved the sack at me. It couldn't still have the water gun in it. It just couldn't. You can't have water guns in school. Patrick had to know that.

He got on the chair where Dawn Marie had been standing and looked down at us.

"Big deal," Dawn Marie said, like it wasn't.

"Shhhhh," I told her.

"It's my day to water Jack's bean stalk," he told Mrs. Zookey. He held his mouth funny when he said it.

She smiled and nodded.

Jack's bean stalk is this plant that sits on the

windowsill. It grew really fast out of a bean we planted the first week of school. Every day we took turns watering it and seeing how tall it was.

Mrs. Zookey had taped a little paper boy in a pointed green hat to one of the branches. That was Jack. At the top of a long stick she had taped a paper giant. He was waiting for the bean stalk to reach him. Dawn Marie said when the plant got up to the giant, he would say "Fee fi fo fum." Then he would climb down and eat Jack up. Every day the bean plant grew some more.

"You want to see how I'm going to water it?"

Patrick whipped his yellow super squirt gun out of the plastic sack.

"He wouldn't dare," Dawn Marie said.

"Patrick Olimpia," Mrs. Zookey called, "you put that down this minute." She jumped up and started toward him.

Patrick did not put it down. He aimed straight at the bean stalk and pulled the trigger. A big, fat stream of water flew all the way across the room. It hit the pot and knocked the whole thing, plop, off the windowsill.

The pot landed upside down. It broke in two pieces. Wet dirt leaked out the middle and onto the floor.

Everybody stared at the broken bean stalk.

"Patrick," Mrs. Zookey said, "you are in big, big trouble."

Patrick *was* big, big trouble.

"You killed Jack!" Linda yelled.

"But he got the giant, too, Dawn Marie said. "That makes him a giant killer."

Patrick looked at Ben and me and smiled a little smile.

I yelped.

Ben sucked in his breath.

Patrick's smile had changed. His teeth were long and sharp and yellow-green. They were fangs. Our bat must have bit him. Patrick was a vampire.

## 5.

# He's a Pest

"Patrick," Mrs. Zookey said, "this is just too much."

Patrick opened his mouth and took out his teeth. They were glow-in-the-dark plastic fangs. He was a fake vampire.

Mrs. Zookey held out her hand. "I'll take that squirt gun. You can't bring it to school. You should know that."

"He knows what he knows," Ben said, and he laughed.

I didn't laugh. Patrick hadn't brought it to school by himself. I had helped.

Patrick hugged it. "It's only water," he said. "I wanted everybody to see how good I could shoot."

"The bean stalk is broken," Linda told us, holding it up. "And you did it." She stuck out her tongue at Patrick.

"I thought everyone would laugh," he said.

Nobody was laughing.

Patrick hugged the squirt gun tighter. His bottom lip was shaking.

He must have filled the big yellow water tank extra full. Squirting the plant hadn't made it empty. Water was dripping out. It was leaking all over Patrick.

Linda saw it first. Patrick's pants were getting wet. A puddle was growing at his feet.

She began to laugh.

Wet pants are funny. Ben and I laughed, too.

Patrick looked down and saw the big wet spot. He tried to wipe it off with his sleeve.

"It's only water," Ben said, just the way Patrick had.

"Serves him right," I whispered. "You know why? Last night that gun wet my bed."

Ben started to laugh again. Me, too. We couldn't stop, even when Mrs. Zookey said, "That's enough, boys."

Patrick gave Mrs. Zookey the water gun.

"Patrick," she said, "you are a good boy. But spraying the plant with water was not good. Bringing that water gun to school was not good. It's against the rules."

"I'm sorry," he said. "I didn't know." He looked at me.

Patrick was new. Maybe he didn't know.

But I gave him the water gun on the bus, so he had to bring it to school. Would he say it was all my fault?

"I will write your mother a note," Mrs. Zookey told Patrick. "I will tell her what you did. I will tell her that you must never, ever bring the water gun to school again. And now I want you to pick up the mess you've made."

I waited for Patrick to say it was my fault, not his. But he went straight to the bean stalk and tried to fix it. He couldn't. Jack and the giant were both stuck in the mud. All he could do was scoop the whole thing into the trash.

"You must stay in from recess for three days, Patrick," Mrs. Zookey went on. That was bad. Nobody wanted to miss recess.

Ben still couldn't stop laughing.

I poked him with my elbow.

Mrs. Zookey looked hard at us and said, "I may have to change my seating chart today." That meant she might move Ben or she might move me. Not sitting together wouldn't be funny at all.

"Now, let's get some work done. I'd like you to finish your endangered animal pictures before recess," she said. "Who needs help?"

Patrick sat down at Table One. He put his head on his desk. I wondered if he was mad at me.

"Richard," Mrs. Zookey said. "I don't see you drawing."

I had to draw a picture of my whale and put it up on the big map of the world.

Ben crunched up his paper. "My baboon always looks like a gingerbread man," he said. "I can draw a really good rat, but my dad says they aren't endangered. Besides, he told me, nobody wants to save the rat."

"It's a pest," Linda explained. "Nobody likes a pest."

"I bet you don't know what animal I'm doing," Dawn Marie said.

"Panda." I remembered. "You told us Friday."

"I changed my mind." She took a brown crayon from the crayon pot and began to draw.

At Table One everybody was drawing but Patrick.

I took a gray crayon and started my humpback whale.

"Guess what. People eat whales," I told Table Two.

"Big deal," Dawn Marie said. "I ate French fried caterpillars once in Mexico. They tasted a lot like Chee-tos." Dawn Marie had been to Mexico, so maybe it was true.

"When I was a baby I took a bite of my mom's lipstick," Linda said. "I thought that's what she did with it. They made a video of me and my teeth are all red."

"Gross," I said, because it was.

Ben leaned over and took a green crayon from the pot. He bit off the tip and crunched it with his front teeth.

"This is how Lettuce chews," he said. When he opened his mouth his teeth looked green and moldy.

"Gross," I said again, because they were.

"Ben, you know better than that." Mrs. Zookey was standing right next to Table Two.

Ben looked down at the table. He shut his mouth tight so his teeth wouldn't show.

"I think," she said, looking us over, "we need to make a change here. There is too much silliness going on and not enough work. Ben, I want you to go to the sink and clean your teeth. Then gather up your things and move them to Table One."

Ben stood up and hung his head. You could tell he knew he'd done a dumb, baby thing.

"There isn't any room here," Joshua called from Table One.

"Well, we'll just have to make room," Mrs. Zookey said. "Patrick, I think perhaps you should change, as well. Gather up your supplies and move them to Table Two."

Linda and Dawn Marie looked at each other.

"Oh, no," Linda whispered. "Not Patrick. We don't want Patrick. He's a pest."

# 6.
## You Can't, It's Mine

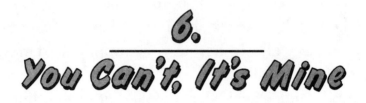

**B**en sat down at Table One with Yolanda and Joshua and Sara. Right away they were having a good time. You could tell. They looked like friends.

Patrick sat down in Ben's old chair. He put a book on his lap to cover the big wet spot on his pants.

"I didn't know you'd *squirt* it," I told him. "I really didn't. Are you going to tell on me?"

He looked surprised. "You didn't do anything," he said. He wasn't going to tell.

Nobody was laughing. Table Two was not the same.

"What's your animal?" Dawn Marie asked him.

Patrick suddenly stopped looking sad. "This is," he told her, and he slipped the fangs back into his mouth. Mrs. Zookey hadn't taken them away.

Dawn Marie rolled her eyes. Linda did, too.

"I'm doing the bat," he said with his mouth full. "I got a bat book from the animal shelf."

Dawn Marie looked up. "Oh, no you're not," she told him. "The bat's mine." She held up the picture she'd been drawing. It looked like a bug with big flappy wings.

"No fair," Patrick said, pulling out his fangs. "I had it first."

"I already made my picture." Dawn Marie waved it in the air. "Where's yours?"

"I've been busy," he said.

"Busy being bad," Linda told him.

He made a face at her. Patrick may know a lot, but he doesn't know much about making friends.

"What do you want to do bats for?" I asked them. "They're pests."

"Are not," Dawn Marie said. Under her picture she printed in big purple letters KITTI'S HOG-NOSED BAT. "It's a teeny, tiny bat. Its body is the size of a jelly bean."

"Bogus," Patrick told her. "Bats are the size of mice."

"This one isn't," she said.

Patrick started to get up, but his pants were still wet, so he sat back down and raised his hand. "Mrs.

Zookey," he called. "Mrs. Zookey, Mrs. Zookey, Dawn Marie took my animal."

"Patrick," Mrs. Zookey said, "you are already skating on very thin ice."

Dawn Marie stood up, walked to the bulletin board, and thumbtacked her picture to the map. "That's Thailand," she said. "My bat lives there."

"Mrs. Zookey!" Patrick called again, waving his arm. "I chose the bat. The bat's mine. I want the bat bad."

Mrs. Zookey sighed. She brushed her hair back from her eyes. "There are quite enough bats to go around," she said. "If you can choose a different endangered bat than Dawn Marie's, I say, go for it. Bats need all the friends they can get."

Then she turned back to the kid at her desk.

"I don't want to be their friend," Patrick said. "I just want to say how they're dying dead as dinosaurs."

"Are *you* going to be a bat's best friend?" I asked Dawn Marie.

"Sure," she said. "I like them. My Kitti's hog-nosed bat eats bugs. That's good. The bats that live around here do, too."

"If you hate them so much," Linda asked Patrick, "why don't you just pick something cute—

like the panda. It's black and white and fuzzy and Dawn Marie isn't doing it anymore."

"I pick bats," he said, "because they're the ugliest and the scariest of all."

"You don't know anything," Dawn Marie told him. "I've got two bats at home and I know."

"Two bats? Ha! You do not."

"Do, too."

"You've got two real live bats at your house? Right," Patrick said, like he knew it wasn't.

"Right," she told him, like she knew it was.

"Do you keep them in cages?" I asked her. "Are they pets like Ben's gerbils?" I didn't believe her either. "You can't have a bat for a pet unless you're a witch or a monster."

"You can come and see them if you want to," Dawn Marie said. "After school."

"Are you making this up?" Linda asked her.

"Come and see. But you've got to promise to be very, very quiet."

"Can I bring my super squirt gun?" Patrick asked her. He was grinning.

"Sure," she said, smiling back. "If Mrs. Zookey will give it to you. And if all you do is wet your pants with it. You shoot my bats, though, and you are one pickled Patrick."

"Ha!" he said. He held up his book. *Extremely Weird Bats*, it was called. "I'm going to find out how weird they are."

"You're weird, too," Linda said, leaning toward him. "You never wear sneakers. Everybody else does."

"My mother wants me to dress like a gentleman," he told her.

"You don't act like one," Dawn Marie said. "You talk like you know it all, and you don't know beans. You sure don't know beans about bats." She got up, walked over to the reading corner, and plopped down in the old bathtub filled with pillows.

"And that goes double for Richard," she called.

We used to be friends at Table Two. No more.

"I know what you're trying to do," Patrick told her. "You're trying to make us mad so we won't come over to your house. But my friend Richard and I, we're coming. And you better watch out what you show us. Richard and I know *all* about bats."

Dawn Marie slid so far down in the tub you could only see her feet.

"Patrick," Mrs. Zookey said, "you are using your outdoor voice and you are clearly inside."

He put his fangs back in his mouth, picked up his bat book, and started to read.

39

"And, Patrick," Mrs. Zookey went on, "I want you to be thinking of something you can do for the class. Something to take the place of our fallen Jack and the bean stalk."

## 7.
# Hanging Out Upside Down

"**Y**ou could take worms to school," I told Patrick. "I know where you could find some. You could fill a jar with dirt and the whole class could watch them wiggle. It wouldn't cost anything."

"Maybe. But it's not as good as a bean stalk. Besides, they'd look out of the jar and kids would feel sorry for them. Run faster, can't you, Richard?"

"Look," I told him, "I don't much want to go to Dawn Marie's." I slowed down and caught my breath.

We'd met on Patrick's corner and we were running the two blocks to Dawn Marie's house. I knew where she lived. I'd been there for a birthday party.

"But she said we didn't know beans about bats," Patrick said. "And we do. We saw a bat. We've got to show her."

"She said double for me," I told him.

"Right. You and me against Dawn Marie. You know that bat book?" he asked me. "I read a lot of it. Being inside at recess isn't all that bad."

I slowed down more.

"Where's Ben?" Patrick asked.

"Still at school. He's helping catch Lettuce. She got loose. Ben's brother blew and blew his whistle, but she wouldn't come."

"You could have stayed and helped," Patrick said.

"Ben asked Joshua to," I told him. Already Ben had a new friend at Table One. And I had Patrick. Him and me against Dawn Marie.

"Why doesn't Dawn Marie like me?" Patrick asked.

"You said her scabs weren't real," I told him.

"I bet," he said, "if her bats are real, they're real *plastic* ones that bounce up and down on a rubber band."

"Ha!" I said. It felt good. I said it again. "Ha!"

"Ha!" he said back, and we laughed.

Linda was waiting for us at the corner.

"Dawn Marie says for us to go down the alley to her backyard. She says I should check out your water gun first."

"I threw it in the trash at school." He showed her his empty hands.

"Did Mrs. Zookey make you?" I asked him.

"No. She told me I could take it home. But it leaked," he said. "Besides, it made people mad."

"My mother said I couldn't have one ever," I told him.

"Well, it's a good thing you don't have water guns," Linda said, "because Dawn Marie told me you couldn't come near her bats if you did."

"This is a joke, isn't it?" Patrick asked her.

"I don't know," Linda said. "She told me it was a big surprise."

We followed her down the alley to Dawn Marie's backyard.

Dawn Marie was waiting for us inside the gate with her arms crossed.

"Promise to be quiet?" she asked. "Lock your lips and throw away the key?"

"Promise," we said, all three of us. We locked our lips. We threw away the keys.

"Cross your hearts?"

We crossed them.

"Come with me." She didn't head toward her house. She led us to a shed at the back of the yard. When she got to the door, she put her finger to her lips.

Patrick rolled his eyes. I thought for a minute he would say, "Ha!" but he didn't. He had locked his lips and crossed his heart.

Dawn Marie opened the door, and we all three followed her into the shed. The windows were dirty and there wasn't much light. I didn't see a cage. I could see some metal chairs. There were lots of pieces of wood stacked in the corner. I saw a bicycle, a baseball, and two bats.

"*Bats!*" Patrick said, pointing and laughing.

I laughed, too. I got the joke. So did Linda. All the time Dawn Marie was being funny. She had *baseball* bats.

"Shhhhhhhhh!" Dawn Marie hissed. "I ought to make you go home."

That was OK with me. I didn't want to be there. It was dark and it smelled like a moldy old basement. I started for the door.

"But," she went on very quietly, "I'll give you one more chance. I want you to see them because you don't believe me. Look."

She pointed up into a dark corner of the shed. Something was there—blobs, small dark blobs. They could have been anything. They could have been shadows.

"They are real live bats," Dawn Marie whispered. "My father found them there Saturday. They sleep all day upside down."

"I'm getting out of here," I told her.

"Wait a minute," Linda said. "How do we know that's not just a bunch of cobwebs?"

Dawn Marie thought about it.

"See that pile of stuff on the floor under them," she said. "That's bats' droppings."

"Doo-doo?" Patrick asked.

"If you want to call it that," Dawn Marie said.

I edged closer to the door, but the bats weren't moving—if they *were* bats.

"They eat hundreds and hundreds of bugs every night. One bat can eat six hundred mosquitoes in an hour, so they make lots of droppings. My dad says it's called guano."

"Guano doo-doo?" Patrick asked.

"If you want to call it that," Dawn Marie said.

I didn't like this. "We can't stay," I told her. "I've got to practice the piano."

"Do they drop it hanging upside down?" Patrick asked her.

"Drop what?"

"Drop the guano doo-doo?"

I started to laugh. Everybody else had unlocked their lips. Dawn Marie frowned at me, and so I stopped.

"Well, my father and I sat here and watched them a long time yesterday," she told Patrick. "Most of the time, you know, they just hang out upside down. But sometimes they'll flip around and hold on with the tips of their wings. That's when they go. The guano drops straight down and they don't get dirty."

"Wow," Patrick said.

"Wait a minute," I told her, "you were sitting in the dark. You couldn't see anything."

"Your eyes get used to the dark," she said. "But sometimes, for a minute or two, we turned on a light." She walked over to a shelf and picked up a flashlight. She pointed it up and then she turned it on.

It made a circle of light on the ceiling. She moved the circle slowly to the corner. One of the blobs moved. It wasn't a shadow. It wasn't a cobweb.

Suddenly it was gone. Its wings were flapping faster than a bird's. It whirled in the air quick, but quiet.

Dawn Marie tried to follow it with her light. I could hardly breathe.

It was one of Dawn Marie's bats.

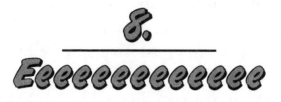

## 8.
## Eeeeeeeeeeee

"Yuck! I can't believe you took us in there," Linda said. "That was mean. I thought you were my friend."

"Can I go back in?" Patrick asked.

We were outside, breathing hard, staring at the closed shed door.

"Do you like them?" Dawn Marie asked him.

"I mean it was *really* mean," Linda said.

She was right, too. It was like Dawn Marie didn't care if we got vampires in our hair.

"They're very gentle," Dawn Marie told her.

"They're bats," Linda said. "I'm going home. I'm going to watch 'Kamikaze Killer Bees' on TV." She slammed the gate when she left.

"How come you want to go back in?" I asked Patrick. "You told me bats give you fangs."

"That's dumb," Dawn Marie said. "They're just little brown bats. I mean, that's what they're called—little brown bats. Their real name is *Myotis lucifugus*. My father told me. It's Latin."

"*My-o-tis lu-ci-fu-gus*. That sounds like a dinosaur name," Patrick said.

"Aren't you scared?" I asked her. "What if they grab your neck?" I scratched a bump on my ankle. "Or your leg?"

"That Dracula stuff is as fake as the tooth fairy," she said.

"You mean there *isn't* a tooth fairy?" Patrick asked. And they both laughed.

"You believe her?" I asked him. "But you know all about bats."

"I read more about them today," he said. "I read they won't turn you into anything."

"Yesterday you made me hide," I told him. "Today you say they're OK."

"Come look again," Dawn Marie said. "We won't touch them. Nobody's going to get bit." She opened the shed door and tiptoed back inside. Patrick went, too. I could hear them whisper.

If I didn't go in they'd think I was chicken. So

I hopped five small steps, ran three, held my breath, and followed them. I also put my hands on my cap so it couldn't be a bat landing field.

Dawn Marie flashed her light on. The bats were both there, hanging on.

"They're my Yummy for tomorrow," she whispered.

That was funny, because, if Mrs. Zookey had called on me, a bat would have been my *Yucky*.

"Do they really have knees that bend backward?" Patrick asked. She nodded.

"They'll leave soon," she whispered. "They go where it's warm in the winter."

"They hibernate," Patrick said, "like bears. I read about it today."

"My dad says they're male bats," Dawn Marie told us.

"Right," Patrick said. "Female little brown bats live in big colonies with their babies. If those were females there'd be *hundreds* of them."

"You know more than beans now," Dawn Marie said.

"I know what I know," he told her.

"How soon?" I asked. "How soon will they leave? Like in ten minutes, or what?" I wanted to get out of there before they did.

Patrick opened one of the folding chairs and stood on it for a closer look. Dawn Marie clicked on her light. I closed my eyes and waited for the bat attack.

"Why don't you just get a ladder and catch one and pet it?" I asked him. "If you think they're so great and you think you're so brave?"

"They'd bite him, that's why," Dawn Marie said.

"You said they wouldn't bite," I told her.

"If you don't bother them they won't. You pick up a bat and you'll scare it. You scare a bat and it'll bite you."

"It's a wild animal," Patrick whispered.

"I petted one yesterday and it didn't bite me," I said.

"You touched it with some grass," Patrick said. "Anyway, I told you not to."

One of the bats swooped near us. Then it flew up to another corner of the shed. I made myself small into a ball.

"Don't *worry*," Dawn Marie said. "It doesn't think you're good to eat."

"But he can't see me. He could hit me by mistake," I whispered. "He's blind as a bat."

The bat flew back to his first corner.

"He is not," Dawn Marie whispered. "He sees very well. And you know what else? What else is that he makes these really, really high sounds that you can't hear."

"Can you hear them?" I asked her.

"No, but the bat does. It goes *Eeeeeeeeeeee* and the sound hits you. And the *Eeeeeeeeeeee* bounces right back to the bat and it knows exactly where you are. It's called echolocation. Even at night when it's totally dark, the bat would know where you are."

I got goose bumps all over. "If it was totally dark I wouldn't be here," I told her.

"He can tell by the sound that bounces off you how big you are," she went on. "If you were a bug he would eat you. If you were you, he'd fly away."

"They're really smart," Patrick said.

She looked up at the corner where the bats were hanging. "I'd do my report on the little brown bat, but it's not on the endangered list."

"You know what kind I'm doing?" Patrick whispered. "It's a flying fox bat. It doesn't eat bugs. It eats bananas and figs and mangoes. It's big. It's five feet across when it flies. I mean, big. You know why it's endangered? It's because people eat it."

"They do not," I said. "You're making that up."

"No, I'm not. I read about it today. People kill it and cook it and eat it up. That's why."

"Euuuuu," I said.

53

"Really?" Dawn Marie asked him. "What's it taste like?"

"They cook it in coconut milk," he told her. "It's *so* big, it's big as a squirrel."

"Mine," Dawn Marie said, "is *so* little, some people call it the bumblebee bat. I don't think anybody eats it."

"I've got an idea," Patrick told Dawn Marie.

"So do I," I said. "My idea is that we leave."

A bat flew down from the corner. It swooped in the air. It didn't want us there. I didn't want to be there.

"If you're going with me, you've got to go now," I told Patrick.

But when I left, Patrick and Dawn Marie were still sitting in the dark shed watching little brown bats.

# 9.
## Bat Bed

Patrick sat in Ben's chair at Table Two. "Was your mom mad?" I asked him. He had a bunch of yellow flowers in his hand.

"She made me bring these," he said, shaking the flowers in my nose. "They stink."

"Is that *all* she did?" I asked him.

"She made me write a letter to Mrs. Zookey saying what a dumb thing I did."

Mrs. Zookey had Patrick put the flowers in a vase. And she thanked him for his letter. But she told him he still had to watch his step.

At Yummy and Yucky time, Mrs. Zookey didn't call on Dawn Marie. I didn't even raise my hand. She called on Joshua, Ben's new friend at Table One.

"Guess what," he said. "Yesterday Ben's gerbil got lost in the fifth grade room. I had this banana left from lunch, and so I peeled it and put it on the floor right where Lettuce ran out. Then I put a shoe box over the banana. I propped it up with this pencil. And when Lettuce ran in for the banana, I knocked the pencil out."

He clapped his hands to show how the box fell. "I caught her."

"Wasn't Joshua great!" Ben said.

"Great," I said.

"That was smart," Patrick agreed.

"I used to have a gerbil," Joshua told us, "but it died."

After school Joshua went to Ben's house. Ben gave him two of his gerbils named Fluffy.

After school Patrick went to Dawn Marie's house. They had a secret project. It had something to do with bats. It didn't have anything to do with me.

I went home by myself. I practiced the piano for fifteen minutes and then I watched "Kamikaze Killer Bees" on TV. I also finished my report on the humpback whale.

On Wednesday at report time, Mrs. Zookey called on me first.

Everybody else sat on the rug. I stood up. I told

about how the humpback whale is forty feet long and humps its back when it jumps. "I never saw a whale," I told them, "and if people don't stop killing them off maybe I never will."

Mrs. Zookey said she learned a lot from my report.

Even before I sat down, Patrick was waving his hand.

So was Dawn Marie.

"I bet they have a big fight," Linda told me, "about who bats first."

Mrs. Zookey said, "All right, Dawn Marie. All right, Patrick. You two are next."

They *both* stood up.

"You first," Patrick whispered. His bow tie was crooked, and he looked a little scared.

Dawn Marie stepped forward. "We're doing our report together," she began. "It's on bats. My bat is one of the smallest in the world. It weighs less than a dime. Its name is Kitti's hog-nosed bat." She held up her picture.

"Pig bat," Linda said. "Piggy."

Mrs. Zookey put her finger to her lips and Linda stopped talking.

"Bat mothers only have one or two pups a year. But some of them live to be thirty years old. A lot of bats are endangered."

Then Patrick held up his piece of paper. His bat picture filled up almost the whole page.

"Mine is the flying fox bat," he said. "It's big. Its body can be as big as a squirrel's and its wings as wide as five feet. The reason why my flying fox bats are almost extinct is because people kill them and eat them," Patrick said.

I raised my hand. "That's not true, Mrs. Zookey, is it? People don't eat bats."

"You told us people were killing whales to eat them," Mrs. Zookey said.

"Yes, but that's different," I told her.

"My Kitti's hog-nosed bat is getting to be extinct," Dawn Marie said, "because people are cutting down the trees near their caves. And that makes the bugs they eat go away."

"I read about this cave where lots of bats died," Patrick said. "Kids lit firecrackers inside it. But, see, bats only have a little bit of fat to last them all winter long. So if they get scared and flap around, they use their fat up and they die."

"I've got two bats who live in the shed behind my house right now," Dawn Marie said. "And each one of them can eat six hundred mosquitoes an hour."

She waited while everybody gasped and gagged and said, "Euuuuu, gross." But she looked really proud, like what she had out there was baby kittens drinking milk.

Patrick picked up a plastic grocery sack. I couldn't believe it. It was the one I'd brought his super squirt gun to school in. Maybe his uncle had given him a new squirt gun. He was never going to be able to go to recess again.

Patrick hugged the sack with one arm. With the other hand he held up a different bat picture. "This is a little brown bat. It's the kind that lives in Dawn Marie's shed."

"*Myotis lucifugus*," Dawn Marie said. "That's its name in Latin."

"So her father . . ."

"So my father," Dawn Marie went on, "he helped Patrick and me build something for them."

Patrick reached in the sack. I ducked. But what he took out was not a squirt gun.

It looked like a birdhouse, but it didn't have a hole for the birds to go in.

"It's a bat house," Dawn Marie said. "My father sawed the wood, but he let us hammer."

"I hit three nails," Patrick said. "This one." He pointed to one on the roof. "This one." He showed us one on the side. "And this one." He held up his thumb. The nail was blue.

"I would say that's fake and he just painted it

59

on," Dawn Marie told us, "but I was there when he hit it."

"Ha," Patrick said. He held up his other thumbnail. It had purple and red stripes painted on it. "This one," he said, "*is* fake."

"He yelled really loud," Dawn Marie told us, "but he didn't cry."

Patrick showed us how the bat house was made. The bottom of it was open. "The bats just fly straight up to go inside. And the wood is rough so they can hold on to sleep."

"Inside there upside down?" I asked.

"And downside up," Patrick told me. "We're going to hang it in Dawn Marie's backyard. We're really near Green Lake where lots of mosquitoes live. So we may get lots and lots of bats to hang out inside."

"How many bats will it hold?" Mrs. Zookey asked them.

"Up to thirty," Dawn Marie told her.

"Thirty!" Linda said. "Thirty bats flapping outside your window all night long! Dawn Marie, I'm never sleeping over at your house again as long as I live. You know what you and Patrick are? You're *batty*."

# 10.

"What are you so scared of?" Dawn Marie asked. "It's just my backyard."

We were all there—Ben and I and Joshua and Linda and Patrick. We wanted to see where the new bat house was going to hang.

"I can't believe you got me here," Linda told her. "What do you want thirty bats for, anyhow?"

"You need exactly thirty bats for stew," Patrick said. And he chased her, waving his arms. "Bat wing stew for me and you. Ha!"

"OK, you guys, let's go look at the ones in the shed." Dawn Marie opened the door.

"I like worms and I like bugs," Ben told her, "but I'm not so sure about bats."

"I'm not going in," Linda said. "It's haunted."

"Me, either," Joshua told her. "Bats turn you into vampires."

"Didn't you listen to *anything* we talked about?" Dawn Marie asked them.

"Maybe they're not so bad," I said. "I think you should call them Wacky and Weirdo."

"It wouldn't do me any good to call them," Dawn Marie told me. "They wouldn't answer." She opened the door very slowly. Linda and Joshua hid behind a tree.

The rest of us tiptoed in. We were quiet as cats. The place still smelled like wet basement. Ben pulled his jacket up around his ears. I held my cap on tight.

We all four blinked until our eyes got used to the dark.

Ben stayed close to the door. "Where *are* they?" he whispered.

Dawn Marie got the flashlight. She turned on the big round beam. We looked in the corner where they had been sleeping. It was empty. We looked in the other corners and up above us, too. Nothing was there.

"I bet they're hiding," Ben said. "I bet they're waiting to dive-bomb us. See you." He opened the door and ran.

No matter where we looked, the bats weren't there.

"Maybe they're out for supper," I guessed. "Maybe they're out gobbling up mosquitoes. I hope they are. Mosquitoes think I'm candy."

"Not dark enough yet," Patrick said.

"It was pretty cold last night," I said. "Maybe they flew away. Maybe they're sound asleep somewhere in their winter cave."

"Yes," Dawn Marie said. "That's just what we said they'd do, and they *did* it. They flew south."

I opened the shed door. "OK, you guys. Come out, come out, wherever you are. The bats have gone away."

"You sure?" Linda asked, coming out from behind the tree.

"That's why I like gerbils better," Joshua said, following her. "You always know where they are. And if they get out you can catch them."

"I know why they went," Ben said. "They went because it's creepy in that shed."

"I bet when they come back they don't move in the new house at all," Patrick said. "The new house doesn't smell like the old one. It smells like pinewood. Besides, it's no fun moving. Things are never ever the same in new places. I know that."

"My dad's going to nail it on the outside of the

shed. That way it'll be easier to watch them."
Dawn Marie pointed to the place. "It'll go right
up near the peak of the roof. He'll have to use a
ladder."

"You know the bat that was in the grass at my
house?" I asked them.

Everybody knew.

"Maybe it was lost then. And maybe now it's in
a cave. And maybe when it comes back in the
spring it will see your new bat house and move
in."

"Maybe," Patrick said.

"I bet in the spring Dawn Marie's two bats will
come back inside the shed," I told them. "And
thirty new bats will move into the new house outside. Then they'll all fly to my yard to eat their
supper." I dug the dinosaur calculator out of my
pocket.

"Some supper," Linda said. "Mosquitoes. Raw.
Yuck."

"Listen to this," I went on. "Dawn Marie's two
bats plus the thirty new ones, that's thirty-two.
And each bat can eat six hundred bugs an hour.
Right?"

Dawn Marie nodded. "That's what the book
said."

I punched 32 × 600 = . "That's *nineteen thou-*

*sand two hundred* bugs chewed up in one hour. *Nineteen thousand two hundred* mosquitoes who won't be chewing me." I couldn't believe it. Bats were the best.

"You know what I'm going to do?" I told them. "I'm going to get my own bats. I'm going to build me a big bat apartment house for my backyard."

"I'd rather get mosquito bites," Joshua said.

"And then there'll be the other one," Patrick said.

"What other one?" Ben asked him.

"I'm making a bat house for school," Patrick said. "Mrs. Zookey told me it could take the place of Jack and the dead bean stalk."

"Yuck," Linda stuck out her tongue. "Hang it far away. I don't want any bats bending their knees backward over me."

"Mrs. Zookey says we'll decide in the spring where to hang it," Patrick told us.

"This is great," I said. "Bat houses all over! We're going to build the Little Brown Bat Capital of the Universe. All summer they'll eat gazillions of bugs. My calculator can't even count that high."

"If we build lots of houses for them and the bats come," Patrick said, "the town won't have to spray for mosquitoes, and people won't have to hang bug zappers in their yards."

I scratched the itchy bite on my ankle. "Patrick," I said, "you're smart."

Patrick smiled. He straightened his bow tie.

"And while we're waiting for the bats to come back in the spring," he said, "I tell you what we're going to do."

"No thanks," Linda said.

He dug something out of his pocket. "I've got these beans. My mom gave them to me."

He opened his hand and showed us. He had three beans with spots on them. "You don't see beans like these every day. Tomorrow we're going to plant these in the ground outside Mrs. Zookey's room. And they'll grow into a bean stalk as tall as the school and taller."

"They will not," Dawn Marie said.

"Maybe not, maybe so," I told her.

"And in the spring," he went on, "we'll hang my bat house at the top of that bean stalk. And lots and lots of bats will come."

"Right," I said. "And there'll be a giant on top. He'll be the giant of *Myotis lucifugus,* the Little Brown Bat Capital of the Universe."

Patrick smiled even more. "These are *very* special beans." He held them out so everyone could see.

"Not," Dawn Marie said.

"I know what I know," Patrick told her.

Maybe Patrick knew beans, and maybe he didn't. Patrick knew bats. And that was good. But, one thing I knew. We still had to watch out.

Patrick was trouble.

# About the Author

Jamie Gilson is the author of more than a dozen novels about funny things that happen to kids in the Midwest, where she has always lived. Her most recent title is *Itchy Richard*, also about the adventures of Table Two in Mrs. Zookey's second-grade classroom. A graduate of Northwestern University's speech school, Ms. Gilson taught junior high school, wrote and directed educational radio and television programs for the Chicago public schools, wrote commercials for fine arts radio station WFMT, and wrote films and filmstrips for Encyclopedia Britannica Films. For ten years she was a columnist for *Chicago* magazine. She and her husband live in a suburb of Chicago. They have three amazing children.